BLACK LAVENDER MILK

ISBN: 978-1-955992-57-2
Book Cover Art: Photo courtesy of Angel Dominguez.
Book Cover & Interior Design: Sarah Gzemski

Published by Noemi Press, Inc.
A Nonprofit Literary Organization.
www.noemipress.org.

BLACK LAVENDER MILK

10th anniversary edition

angel dominguez

A Fragmentary Forward of Light to Re-open the Dzonot

(Black Lavender Milk, 10 years later)

10 years seeking. 10 years seaming. 10 years applying heat to the tectonics so as to emerge from within the cenote cradling memory, meaning, and the ancestors.

We return now, not fractured, but wholly aware that *Black Lavender Milk* continues to tend to the dreamgardens of possibility. The depths remain widening, and as such, a constellation of five seers provide this new edition the architecture to enter this palace of prisms.

Light. Light. Light.
Light light light light.
Light, light.
Light.

~

In your hands is a book rooted in a glass of water. Angel Dominguez plunged into the dzonot as a child, unable to hear the warnings that first time he entered the portal of the Mayan underworld. The poet opened his grandfather's suitcase, "holding charged archival materials and notebooks and dried flowers and love," and dove inside it, down into the memory of a future "standing on a narrow alabaster bridge" that is *Black Lavender Milk*. "A dzonot blossoms where you failed to bury it," and this is the book's tenth anniversary. Our bodies are different. We read it ten years ago, a major occult reveal offered to us by one of the great poets of our time, a poet whose body changed as all our bodies changed, while the poems hold the space of their birth. If we live to be a hundred, the genius of Angel Dominguez will dive into us with a treaty for all future readers, notarized by mirrors dripping from the dzonot.

—CAConrad, author of *Listen to the Golden Boomerang Return*

Like being wedged in the arrangement; like a large blooming cactus, grief taking shape, a turquoise mountain; like beginning to recount; like loosening your hand from its shell; like watching a distant lens pass over (notations of) trees and (scabs of) earth; like standing in the book, a poem, the clipped yellow wick of a candle, a contemplation; like forgetting what you felt before, even as you remember it; like running downstream, slipping on a faint trace of choreography, a blue burst of air; like coyote scat, fumes from a star; like yarn through trees, a faceless brigade; like tongues as big as clouds, and ribs and lungs saturating the page; like image vanishing in language; like a blurry liquid; like sea constricted to earth; like pouring (being poured) in sleep; like dream channeling silence into the body — Xix — like black lavender milk.

—Jacob Khan, author of *Mine Eclogue*

And so we return to the cenote and to the airport, those liminal sites—one magic, one banal—that Black Lavender Milk holds within it. Fitting, for this book is all about return, returning (home)(to Xix)(to the earth)(to the continent). But Dominguez's gambit here is that the return stops at the verb, at the language: *Black Lavender Milk* is "to return." Its portals, its flights, its grief are all cyclical, never truly stopping or arriving, always stopping and arriving. Just as Dominguez in *Desgraciado* could only write to the Diego de Landa within the letter itself, not his fleshy double lost to history, here Dominguez summons the water, grandfather, home, within their text and its rituals. In its teary-eyed geomancy, this book caught me many years ago needing respite from my own anxious geometry; it returns to me and finds me no different, but more grateful than before.

—Gabriel Ojeda-Sagué, PhD, author of *Madness*

6 million years ago a benthic thing squinted from the dark waters at the crepuscular melt over this fungal terra of a Chicxulub somnambulism. And gasping out from this sentient ooze the poem was born and made diasporic along the pollination dust of this cosmic amphibious black lavender milk, a wiggle over the phlegm moon, among a drift yawning from the dzonot, as Tzukan smacks in a room of echoes and stalactites branding origins. Evolution in these constellations of somnambulist bestiary, like cloud botanic of a miracle trace, the golden lace winding through us to the first ink drawn from Angel's pen some rotation ago. Since then, some fracture creeping down skull lined clay walls and wind-worn edges later, cafes and nodding donkeys crowd out family homes, through the mute horrors of slow violence in slower gentrification, making a legacy of superfunds and incinerators that exhale pollutions of other colonies into and out of our bodies. And the tired bodies, the longing tongue, and crippled hands know the home spoken in somnambulism. The feel the call and aching warmth of that call. When we swan dive on return to those still waters of Black Lavender Milk dzonot, even experienced divers can lose their way. There are more than one surfaces in that water. Some surface a millennium in the future, 6 million years ago.

—Daniel Talamantes, author of *Ruminate Emergent*

Somnambulism 01.01.2015

You met me in dream on the cusp of a dzonot, one year before the release of Black Lavender Milk.

we enter—i should write this down—through a space calcified by mutual departure. i reach for a glass of water. tenuous and temporary, the dream dissipates, drifting past remains of rafters not yet charred, anticipating the consequences of ash and disregard. horizontal, i slip into lavender submersion.

underground at the edge of the clear unending depth before us. stalactite. cerulean. a hollow echoes into us. floating beneath the mirror, faces turned towards us, eyes sealed shut: the bodies of the dead. abandoning your shoes to the shore, you dive into the void. i cling to the raw traces of our exhaustion. your body cuts the stillness; you cut me unknowing.

you who do not fear deep water but cluster to it. you who archive grief at the edges of sleep. you approach each suspended body, kissing one and then another. one by one their eyes open. rhizomatic, atemporality teases an opening. struggling to surface, you emerge dripping. as you always have. you hand me a manuscript. smudged ink warping white paper. a transcript, you say: the voices of the dead.

— Emji Saint Spero, author of *Disgust*

~

In the illumination, may we see all the years that came before and all the years still to follow.

For every body that (ever) held me.
For Joe.
For Xix.

This is a book of non-memoirs. It is happening right now, it doesn't matter when this now was or is or shall be. It's a book like sleeping deep and dreaming intensely–but there's an instant when you awaken, sleep fades away and only the taste of dream remains in the mouth and in the body, only the certainty of having slept and dreamt remains.

Clarice Lispector,
A Breath of Life (Pulsations)
(trans. Johnny Lorenz)

Do you want to remember your dreams? Pour a glass of water at night. Drink half the glass before bed and remember to drink the other half upon waking–the moment our deep star touches your skin and kindles you to flame: you are a magus. You are a form of water. You are a lot of language. You are blood and salt. Pour the glass of water. From the sunset, from the faucet; from your dream breath. Put a palmful of water to your lips and try to remember why we sleep, why we dream–that we may pass through a portal without shape and awaken elsewhere, older, and here now. Go to bed before you read this book. Carry it with you and don't read it. You're sure to remember if you follow this: gather your sleep, strung together with water, cupped by tongue sound, say it with me now:

How will I know (to meet you) when I arrive?

Sigh a breath to your left and make sure you've kept a pocket full of stones and sand–the sound of ocean water weighs gravity when marked upon the body, doubling seasons; stretch time to fit what you remember. Meet me in the orchard, or airport.

Vestibule A: Appendix I

I write the book before falling apart; I fall with the pages. I sway with the dirt. I coddle the failure until it's become a bird. Until it crashes in field. Until it's become erased. Until it becomes, until.

The sentences are creaking with the way they're holding water. The weight disbursed between the book and the body holding the book. I build a tension to let go. I forget how we approach writing and start writing what's missing. I get lost and tell no one. I let the book sink until it's become another form of emptiness. I'm more interested in its lack.

The scene erodes with a violet fragility. I soak in a bath of rose petals; the water goes from pink to dark bruise. I lose track of the continent I'm writing in. I forget the frame of the novel; the language grows wild. I give up haunting all my failures. I work them into my skin, like a poem. I burn the book so many times the manuscript exists as a form of condensation–the sky opens up and pours out a book you'll never read. I wish I could still speak it. I wish I could remember what we say. Every yesterday piles itself into a dendritic agate pose. In repose, the novel writes itself into my sleep. I dream of many airports but never a plane. I say the word sky and the window becomes a doorframe. I don't have the strength to pick up the phone. The book is dead and I'm dragging its entrails across a continent. I smash the book against my face and weep when I can't read the words. "Our longing is our legitimacy," that's what Cecilia (Vicuña) told me, documenting detritus from a Colorado summer creekside performance. Several people die in the writing of this novel, or, they died while this novel is (being) written. I lack a language to communicate. I wish I could tell you the color and breath of a flower. I wish I could explain lavender to you. I make a dark midnight from the sound of my living.

I boil water and shed from stress. Infinite realities, blurring. In one, I am two centimeters to my left. Nothing comes together and every archival component fails. I forget what I'm talking (to you) about.

The book stops writing and dreaming feels further away. I interrupt (myself) (with) living. I have visions of bodies on beaches holding flares–it's sunset, but that's not important. When the book is not happening, I find time trickling in through my wrist; I resist the urge to be(come) specific. I dream the novel upon landing. The novel was never a novel but an orchard; the manuscript was always just a hole in the ground. The sun snows until the rain overtakes the creek in a flood. I abandon the book under the cover of escape; I make my way, sniffing a lilt sky for signs of light; a dim become bright.

The language exhausts itself in the repetition of thinking; before reading, you should know I thought of all of these words for weeks and pages and planes and places until I could finally open my mouth. But something like flowers comes out. Something like a thick light of lavender milk. I am dreaming right now. We burrow home into our blood. In the house of your heart you start a small fire to bring back with you. The continent rains for 10,000 days and nothing ever gets done. The book grows roots in a glass of water. The somnambulist drinks nothing but white light, and wine. Grass grows thick in the cottage of your liver and you try to drown the weeds out with color. You saturate the rhythm(s) of your blood until there is continuity. Like veins. You recall becoming a river. You recall swimming against the current until there was no strength left in you and the river drowned in your memory. You wake up six months later to find yourself still grieving a site where your paw marked a grave; you read the language but don't understand. You make the gestures but the movement is all wrong. You stop writing.

I forget how to write and give up before the book is written. Your hand touches a semblance of time; you remember the scent of 3 a.m.–locate the ocean with(in) your tongue. I keep writing (through) exhaustion until I write something else instead.

I wake up with a sprig of sun stuck in my lungs. I cough lavender and form visions from the obstructions. I try to remember my dreams, but often I remember a big black nothing – the lack of image, the unconscious meandering void.

It's several days until I am finally able to bring myself back to myself to write anything down. The dream falls through the window and pollen corrupts it. My eyes grow red with heavy light waves; the blood thickens; my lips become dry.

In the daylight that presents itself beyond us, there is the inevitable; we try our best to hold on to the hope of it.

I retrieve the residue of a dream and ruin my skin with sunlight. Sometimes we are flying over the moon, and its desert - this flight is as long as you want it to be.

The pollen piles up upon the sidewalks and buries the asphalt. The smell of 3 a.m.; it never leaves. I teach myself new words by pondering your dreams where we (might) meet. Quiero limpiar el libro con mi lengua, pero soy sonambúlo y no se como entender la escritura. My watch keeps breaking. I wake up and it's missing, a small scar sleeping in its place. I disclose a syllable you're not used to saying, though I've said it like a prayer all my life: Xix.

I wilt a rose between my teeth and go (back) to sleep. I wanted to talk to you about dzonots, and what they mean.

What does it mean to become a dzonot?

I return to the orchard before the book is finished, to find you. Seems we've fallen asleep in this deep valley heat. Xix. I keep imagining this moment in which the book or rather, the introductory essay on dzonots arrives. This never happens, the words won't emerge and I never feel ready to write the thing. I write instead about how it's been over 10 years since I felt their cool abundance, the way they held my body, cradled beneath the earth. Every dzonot holds its own myth, its own history, and its own power. It's said that every dzonot has a guardian; this guardian acts as a protector or spirit of the dzonot. You're not supposed to enter a dzonot after dark. But I've been trying to form a dzonot from ribbons of night and the atoms of dreams. I've been attempting to communicate something else, outside of our world. Dzonots are portals to Xibalba, the Yucatec Maya underworld. Here, the bodies from which my blood originates would toss offerings, or offer themselves in hopes of invoking a livable future. Sometimes, a body would emerge from the waters with a message from below. Dzonot is one indigenous spelling of the Spanish word: Cenote. These portals are holes in the limestone foundations of the peninsula; they are all interconnected with water – their rhizome leads to the coast;

touches Tulum. I remember my first dzonot. We saw a small hand-painted sign that read: DZONOT, with a black arrow pointing off the road. We followed the sign to a clearing in the surrounding jungle. There were no bodies present. I bolted from the car, running towards what looked like a vast hole in the earth; my family yelled for me to stop what I was doing. But I was an American then, hot-blooded and ignorant; I ran until I had to jump. It was far deeper than I realized and I screamed, falling into one of Xibalba's many mouths. *¡Que Salvage!* They shouted; you could have died! The water was clearer than any memory could possibly reproduce; I could see straight to the bottom of the dzonot floor, where I had been warned, underground river-currents c/would catch hold of me; I could drown, or be spit out in a dzonot hundreds of miles away, without any way of knowing where I was. I could get lost in Xibalba and never return. I never did dive down to find out if this was true. I knew dzonots were places of power. I remember every member of my family telling me about the magic of their water; how anyone who drinks the water of a dzonot would be bound to return to the peninsula based on taste alone. The taste of home. I keep waiting to arrive at a point in my life where the air is hot and thick with ancestral-familiarity, where I stare back into portal or a space of recollection, clear as sky.

I don't want to write a novel anymore.

I built you a dzonot instead: an airplane window glimpse of Xibalba.

I want to stop writing the book now, before you read it.

Gather Yr Sleep

I return to the orchard in dreams. The land grown wild with distance; time smudged violet, the citrus trees give off a dim aura; years of night left, scattered. I cycle my blood through these words.

Aisle memory: when I was young, I could not sleep. There was never enough night in me; he died before his birthday: a swaying eucalyptus breath lifts body from bed and exits out the window, leaving behind a single avocado.

I am trying to remember what we say.

We communicate in phase; I phrase my body that you might

see its language; maybe you're on this flight too.

I ran for a week without water, running for Wyoming only to wake up in a departure zone. I needed to go home. Find an orchard of my own. The oranges have grown dim in memory.

Once, made a light.

Once, built a flower without water. The cactus knew what to do when he disappeared; after he left, we found a flock of flowers blooming up the night palm on every full moon.

Night bruises: I see patches of the orchard wilting through. A return ticket has curled and blackened edges. Not from fire, but time. The language disappears.

Omissions may lead you astray, following along with you.

I try to

Some one always dies. A reason to go anywhere—to disappear into a p(a/o)st tense until appearing suddenly at the precipice of the ocean—in someone else's dream(s). Outside: birds fly; I cannot tell what time it is.

Won't you wear this fingerprint?

I could never run far or fast enough to leave.

Waiting angles hold a suitcase, I remember his wooden case—
that hot day—I thought we'd never leave, (still) afraid of when
I'll wake up upon landing.

To be empty.

To learn the space it holds.

Dreams spill into Mobius strips & smoke on water persists. To wake up tired: trying to remember how it was when I was older.

I go running into November.

The wind came and took the leaves away.

When there were only branches, it began to snow; this stops my running—asphyxiated asthmatic reaction dilating the time of the heart. It does not snow in the Yucatán. I wake up sweating in a hammock on the front porch of my notebook. Afraid I might forget.

Running weaves a speak of time between breathing.

A dim becomes a bright. Night beckons body to motion. Moon calls to sun in particle exchanges that fringe blue amongst mountains.

Hearing aircrafts depart or land; is one for me? I run for the nearest exit. A dim shot in the dark finds a means to become a bright. Running right up the mountain hoping to catch a blue of wind.

Tickets torn by faceless figures, falling, line follows periphery. The overhead temporary. The opens close.

Bodies wait in silence, no one turning. Only slight fidgets of the arms and legs as the procession continues.

Having almost missed my flight, I arrive at the back of the line, lights off in the aircraft ahead of me; most bodies in seats are asleep.

It's still too early to see.

Something like time sent tilted pink skies across time: mountain coastline: I learned to build ocean out of mirrors and salt water—red soil for flavor—the Rocky Mountains were once an ocean; I pluck a chunk of Quartz from the earth and place it in my mouth. Am I writing "a novel" now? I am feral, coyote beneath, pink sky singing Kunzite.

I keep a jar of water next to me while sleeping.

My grandmother told me this was a Mayan method of capturing your dreams—the trace trapped in a molecule—something inside of you recalls the blue before it happens and, oh look: the sun. Photons fall like leaves underwater—the dream slows time. Lungs dilate at the first sip; I take notes that appear elsewhere, in other (note)books.

Sit near an exit...

Do you understand your responsibility?

Open the exit with both hands when the time comes.

Enjoy your flight.

Adrift in a swamp of feral residue, phonons limping along, eyes closed, trying to remember running—trying to do something to take my mind off leaving. I almost wrote living. I think I meant living.

Sometimes I go running for miles without stopping. Until my lungs are a pale blue fire and my heart smells of blood, and salt. Sometimes I run until I can smell the ocean in Colorado, one thousand miles from it.

I empty out the stones.

When the sea-shelf disintegrates here, there is night—the mountains release their dims, clouds become bright. There is a continent within my body that becomes clear.

A space where there may be departure and retrieval; slow, peristaltic fidgets of time.

I spent the morning picking out gravel from my palms.

Extracting the darker parts, cleaning out the flesh.

I think I fell while running last night. I,

recalled falling in(to) the Yucatán.

Into a ten-meter void that ended with water.

I went running straight into what was missing in the earth.

Some Notes on Forming Dzonots

Some notes on forming dzonots:

Step 1. Locate the event boundary; rub the soil into your skin. Begin digging.

Step 2. ______________________________________.

Step 2a. Make black water: the water my grandfather described to me the morning after he had a vision: milky black midnight, thick; something that smells of salt and blood. His vision was standing on a narrow alabaster bridge in a dark space—no moon—bodies everywhere in the water. I wonder if I too was a body in the void of dream. He didn't know how to help them; the next day there were reports of a tsunami somewhere on the other side of the pacific. We watered the avocados and lemons. We buried salt beneath the orange tree.

Step 3. Stop when you reach your elbow, or shoulder; you'll know when to stop.

Step 4. Equip the hole with a plastic bag membrane: this is not biodegradable and perhaps reminds you of an ocean, or airport.

Step 4a. Continue to make black water: crush charcoal from burnt palm trees; add cold coffee and day old wine. Stir. Continue, adding salt to the liquid—watch for colloidal materials to form a constellation. Add lemon juice for flavor. When the water thickens with memory, begin to pour.

Step 5. Deposit what you remember losing; lower your fingers into the water and retain: rough, yet soft. Hands.

Step 6. Go for a run. Continue until you reach a body of water, or become a body of water.

Step 7. Return home via airplane. Take notes:

A room full of mirrors beckons a body across the void; they voice a portal with(out) outline. Find the route that requires the least oxygen—language cryogen: Xix, I brought you a pint of old blood under the orange tree, drunk off whiskey and trying to bury these notebooks behind me in a time that precedes and haunts me; I want memories to bring (me) back.

Find an earth scab; catch a bit of glass from the nearest car crash, press the substance to skin: hints of then, buried in our blood. A body of night, curved across a planet. Our molecules call across the void and bury sunlight in our sleep; how will I know?

The act of recollection requires a precise temporal orientation; this frames the pyramidal neurons to activate in such a way that they become relevant to the body recalling memory. This does not make a memory "real."

Experiential reality occurs within a quarter of a second of "actual" reality; I am never now, here—always no where running; remembering:

I was asleep on an airplane somewhere above a continent.

I see nothing but pale blue frequencies broken up by scratched Plexiglas and wavering heat rising outside the station. The blue chair was cold. I only want(ed) to rest.

I see nothing but dark road and tethering orange globes, night running floods across Colorado.

Retrieving these vicarious moments from the dark ocean outside airplane: I know them to be half excerpts; all internal.

I think this may be said of all memory:

A body is forgetful.

When my grandfather was a young boy somewhere outside of Mérida, where the air is hot and dzonots line the flat lands, he lived with his mother, brother, and three sisters.

He used to tell me small stories and aisle memories from this space preceding the birth of my mother.

When he was young his family only had tortillas and mantequilla to eat.

Sometimes only tortillas.

His mother sent him away to a church to learn to become a priest; she did this because she knew there was not enough of anything for everyone;

She knew.

When he arrived,

All he wanted was

to go home.

He spent every lunch running off into town trying to shine people's shoes and trying to sell avocados and anything he could in order to return.

It took him three years.

After three years he came home to his mother and family, only, I never heard what happened after—only pits and pieces; that he'd flown on a plane to America, standing; washing out pots bigger than his body in Hollywood; coming home with his nose chopped off in hand, too drunk to go anywhere else; I met him in the after of it all, when he'd become a snowy headed shaman, tending to his garden: roses, lemons, oranges, and avocados, talking to me about the ways in which the heart worked, how the light of the sun could alter its functions; somehow he widened my breathing so that I could run. I remember these constellations of breath while running; running until I feel it in my teeth, pulsing upwards towards my pupils, the dark mirrors through which I am real.

I sit between two sleeping bodies in flight, writing their sleep.

The flight twitches and shakes.

I'm documenting my own.

The ink pools as I pause on my i's and a's—I can't help but remember my grandfather, his departure from home, selling avocados; his running. The way the earth held his ruined knees, slipping on train tracks; gravel in his palms. I blur the space between us further, retracting my pen in favor of my body; I go running through the orchard of my heart; I fall with the rain. I become another wash of mud and water.

My Tía once asked me to chew a piece of charcoal with yerba Buena. I rinsed my mouth out with dzonot water and swallowed black powder shards.

It's said that all who drink dzonot water are bound to return to the Yucatán from the taste alone: the taste of Home.

I'm trying to give you water with this language: to return.

In the air,

I think of charcoal coffee soil water; how I wanted to chew it between my teeth.

I dug three holes in the backyard of my grandmother's home, orchard still fresh on my palms. I dug where there was once a tree.

I filled it with black water, the opposite of dzonot water; I made a pupil. I took notes upon the obsidian mirror of night.

The eye of the airplane window triggers agua negra, 20,000 feet en el aire; I don't know when we're going, to where.

Other Notebooks

Tubes and wires trace and communicate (his) deterioration; (our) bodies archive and endure a sinking.

The bruise became a distance.

The distance grew a shadow; a window grown from sleep may harbor traces of transit. Try to remember why we fly.

I've grown curious as to the programming of the heart, how that vapid organ must feel lucid, in my palms. On the floor. In the detritus of vacant sound, I think of rivers. I remember hearing somewhere that the soothing effect of running water is produced by a flux of negative ions. These are my negative ions, writ in water for you, that we might remember together.

My grandfather taught me to make dzonots:

Pouring water from the avocado hose into a plastic depression in the earth, it was an approximation for memory-skin to be worn. To be sustained. He became citizen that day.

I go to sleep and return exhausted

Water holds memory and I sip from the nearest cup/the sound of it: it rained today. We are a matter of emergency exits and escape routes.

It will rain.

I hold out my body in a running motion hoping to catch a wind wisp of him; I run until I (might) collapse in a bed of November.

Sometimes I let myself fall, just to feel it.

Watching vessels depart from outside of Denver, I am an exhausted dirigible, floating down freeway a(midst) still construction. Leaning on sleep. I gather yr sleep; I hold it in my body like an organ, or scar. It smudges my language clean.

Airplanes are images without gender—and if splayed, they may reveal a bifurcated reality: two aisles of bodies punctuated by space, unable to be distilled to a nationality or tongue—most everyone is quiet during the flight, we the strangers headed west, knowing not and saying nothing. Bodies touch in proximity and this is how we communicate our lonesome feels without looking. Longing to be looking.

I wrote this from after blue

burnt rubber on tarmac,

where we left, off.

An airplane barrels through the continent of night; turbulence is common. Turbulence is not trauma, at least not initially. The body of night ruptures and returns unscathed; I cannot say the same for those who recall what's never happened.

Planetary phenomena: a pair of generational alleles inhabit flat coastal topography; close by there are traces of architecture, proof that someone had been there and lived.

We were on the coast, at the cusp of tomorrow—the last night cycle spiraling into the next light.

Atoms as hovering orbs of golden light: a room of them mapping the monstrous grieving heart. I cut the atoms and made them mirrors. I wove a red thread through every plumed serpent with a horse head; each dzonot formed another puncture wound, another plume of time. I find light grows unstable, smudging bright water, stillness emerges: threads become luminous despite obsidian night. Look into a dark mirror to find your way (home).

Somnambulism(s) I

Despierta Sonámbulo
Y cuéntame Coyote,
la Huerta: como empezó;
tu Xix: un Dzonot

Xix: you were a watchmaker with a jewelry store in downtown L.A.; a dealer in time, you tuned quartzite: 32,768 Hz and whistled for me to follow through the subway. Un bolsa de aguacates, limones, y tres naranjas kept us quiet while waiting to arrive. I've kept every departure: they occupy a small wooden box below blue jars. I want(ed) you to know how I've roamed in search of stones, in search of other portals, in hopes of finding you somewhere with(in) a dream; I'm always trying to blur reality, nodding off into the person next to me, running into me running into me running into 4 a.m. instability. Breaking into an airport; running for the orchard. I remember things that are (not) happening, say, continuing from where we left off: soft syllables made of mud; water, witching up a spell for something like transport, something like continent, something like crystal-memory; I press a tip of quartz to my tongue and run west up mountain, far from the ocean; I still smell salt when there's a hint of blood—I bit my tongue—caught managing a mongrel timeline not fit for linearity: somnambulism(s) last(ing) a flock of years; here I find myself failing to write an orchard, attempting instead: a continent within a dim body, not yet formed and tired from running:

I only want(ed) to arrive.

If you want to follow me to the orchard:

Combine equal parts Citrine and Kunzite petals.

Follow the Moldavite that followed you home.

Follow the dead wherever they may wander.

Follow the notebook until it becomes water.

Combine equal parts exhaustion and atrophy;

A dzonot blossoms where you failed to bury it.

Night grows into the orchard; sleep spreads throughout the oranges and by morning, its memory casts shadow(s).

Xix, before I left—I felt an after approaching–in search of that before-body I fragment, catching curves of descent in the orchard. I watch the sky in my sleep. It breaks off glowing fruit, falling into plastic bags for safekeeping—I keep sleeping to forget. To keep it safe.

I balance 3 blue jars on a shelf in the room I rent:

1. A mixture of Charcoal and raw Kyanite. Ocean.

2. I broke the jar before it could recall what it held: part of my body maybe, a dim start–some memory shard ground up into an Azurite moon.

3. Quartzite variants; rose petals.

I drink from these cups and go running for it.

The sun has not come up, but maybe you know this.

What never happened:

Waiting in slow light, pressurized by our oxygen—dim faces recycle(d) sleep, or are they empty seats?

The flight returns to me in bits and pieces,

as it's happening,

I might be

running 5,831 ft.

Most commercial aircrafts fly at an altitude of 30,000ft.

This notebook is a runway, or entrance, but that doesn't mean anything yet.

Tell me about the moment when you start to dream:

To feel the body feel the body feel: a hypersensitive lucidity.

Horizontal. Then, suddenly vertical. The body confronts intersecting realities with muscle spasm(s). Time regenerates and becomes suspended along with sensory details. For example: there is no sound. The doubling is dizzying—facing both red sheet and dream—an accidental glimpse outside the body: it's raining. Determine a point of entry: between the ribs there is a pile of blood become calcium—dismantle the fossil. Return the body to a state of arrival. The sun is not yet. The rain approaches. The body fidgets; it shakes. The sensation is that of accumulation—the blood of the orchard was once measured with clocks and notebooks until finally the dream dispersed and I found myself smashing my writing, naked in my bed bending mirrors into memories, howling like a hurt animal on the floor of my notebooks—I keep trying to remember where we wake up; when that was.

How will I know when I arrive?

Will you meet me in the orchard?

In the house of your body, you light a candle and leave the windows and doors open.

A single mirror is placed upon the earth, sinking beyond sight; everything remains

this far away.

I still remember falling asleep. How we felt before plucking avocados from the sky. Forming vestibules from the night I, didn't mean to write anything down.

Tell me something about the orchard:

A flock of mirrors were forced from their first home—Hollywood needed parking lots, not poor immigrant dwellings—there was once a family preceding the asphalt smear; they moved to a valley of train tracks, warehouse walls; each month brought european glass from car crashes on the corner—there was a tract of land where they began to dream again; the orchard began and continues to grow when tired mirrors lay sleeping; sometimes we'd wake up with rose petals in our coffee. Sometimes we'd wake up, asleep in the orchard. Night covering our mouths.

Return to the Orchard / La Huerta Empieza

Empieza con la huerta, start (t)here: skin seeks a shore in soil.

You go to sleep to find the orchard, *te acuerdas*?

I remember the way the sun baked my skin brown as we watered the roses; it was near this Virgin de Guadalupe statue that we placed shells. Here, we gathered conches.

We brought the sea back with us and filled the husks with water. We gather petals.

An outline surrounded by echoes of the ocean; the roses have grown into the sound of it, bursting a violent pink scent every May.

Almost asleep, bending timelines into orange-lilt tarmacs and small waiting areas.

Xix slept most of the way.

I ran downtown and up a mountain, found him sleeping in my bloodstream, still smiling as the sun beamed beyond the pink pack of clouds bringing down a soft rain.

I brought these dreams with me in case of evacuation.
In the event we forget, how we continue to arrive.

Sometimes I nod into the person next to it,

saying nothing and falling asleep;

and I fall.

Sometimes I try to say it, in my sleep:

I tried to destroy it: to let it go

I can't.

Notes in Case of Evacuation

I am writing these notes in case of evacuation.

Remove the door with both hands.

Aisle memory: discussing dead bodies, asleep above the soil—bring a palmful of salt; scrub the rock clean, gleam signs of a site that once held another space—one for now absent bones and missing Garnet—the future holds us like night holds the asphalt in a city you've yet to visit.

An avocado seed splits its body in two upon a blue windowsill,
still: I slept in the orchard, until I was certain.

You were gone.

A mask descends from the airplane at the limit of blue: sky fractures into a vacuum despondence; asphalt blurs to void.

The absence of light does not imply a vacancy.

There are no seat rotations on this flight, though you might get up and brush paws with sleeping shadows and outlines.

Luminosity exudes from marrow moving, femur and shin—
the calcium opens:

Blue as an indication of temperature, or

A touch of time

passing.

The air was cold this morning.

I thought I might split my shins.

Then:

a sudden elevation,

a body below

(eee)

dangling in repetition,

enduring.

I thought about running to Wyoming

Folding time from a notebook on sleep

I form an escape route from a vanishing.

The language fails to appear.

How to approach the earth:

With a soft gravity to deepen where we lay.

Opening allows water to seep in.

Water remembers time.

We do not.

I need more time.

I need you
to believe
me.

Evacuation Encantation / Terminal Zero Departure

Empezó la huerta
Con memoria fracasado
Sonambúlo despierta
Los dzonots: soñando

It's 3:45 in the morning.

A body leaves a bed. It does not return.

Subtract the sound, or the semblance of such; it's raining.

The body exits out a door—in a lemon light—I can't tell what time it is. If it is an is or was.

Sometimes I wake up younger. In the orchard taking walks with ghosts, watching petals float towards ocean salt or sky. I might be on the verge of passing out. So tired I can't raise my wrist above my chin without dimming down the tarmac, or notebook; lines that read like falling: light feels different, now.

I don't remember.

I picked up the smudge of the novel; I smeared my face. I asked my dreams, "Can we please get the words out of the blood?" trying to wake up with that language, a scar.

I (still) try.

What never happens: ants fail to bloom a peony; by morning,
a bulb rots darkly after falling dim; lavender evacuates, bright.

When did this scar arrive? Black milk midnight sighed sky
blue until I could not remember how bright the stars were.

Extract a distance from the (dis)coloration of a bruise;
combine a Xix of stars trapped in a blue jar of moon-water.

Was (it) a flock of bodies positioned at right angles or timelines
configured into a distant geometry?

Neural-rivers

in proximity,

humming like

blood slides

in a box.

Waiting releases writing; most of this book is (not) happening somewhere in an airport or transit vehicle; as you're reading, I might be above the continent, reviewing this sentence and wondering how you curved the light into your pupil so gracefully; how you made this language with me, with a hum of blood. There: do you feel it? A Xix.

I wrote this for you in the orchard. I wrote the iron taste of our blood using lemon seeds and orange rinds. I keep breaking my watch against my writing. We take a step. A disembodied voice speaks a string of letters and numbers–remember your emergency exits; remember how we exit, as quietly as we entered. Maybe humming a little lune. Fill a cup.

As you read this, I'm writing something else. The airplane is underwater. Maybe this is about surface(ing) or, below it. Maybe you caught a brief hum of your own; found this book vibrating beneath a bench, or on the shelf of your favorite bookshop, or café. Don't pay for it. Steal it if you can. Like an in flight set of evacuation instructions: slowly slip the language into your notebook(s), try not to notice trembling.

Scientists invented a word for the smell of rain; naming something doesn't mean you can know it; saying the name doesn't make something real. See: Xix xix xix xix xix xix xix xix. I hope you don't see a number. Do you see the problem with naming? Do you see the problems with reading? I meant to write: r e m e m b e r i n g.

What do you remember, about dzonots?

I pluck a dzonot from my heart and offer it as a fingerprint.

If you get caught going through security, know you're safe—I carry you with me. When the moonlight wakes me, you feel a blur about your morning; we're on opposite sides of the world but still our blood's been thinned and threaded together by the site of a flight never taken; that doesn't mean it didn't happen. Don't you remember, what we('ve) said?

I stop writing the novel and flee to find the flight still alive in the cracks of California, far from Colorado where I return to vacant redwood—a vision of ocean I know. I drop the landscape and snow falls across the tarmac—it's September when I fall in love, but really before that, in August; the dream(s) remained unwritten, or unfinished. The flight that never happened began taking on passengers. People read a book you'll never read. The language dissipates like the language from a dream; the book forgets itself and begins again, from the heart of its failure, grizzly, unafraid of death.

Sometimes I catch a glimpse of the book before you're reading it; it's an accident, the way a ghost quivers, the way the sun shines gray, beyond your plane of vision - that reach.

I meet you on your way to the gate; you don't know me but I've been waiting for you, see: we're both asleep right now, maybe that's lost on me, but we're moving through security like blood slides in a box; we're fragile—ready to break, I take my headphones off to greet you. Hello. Won't you wear this fingerprint: it reads: vacant flight memory, overnight blue light. Late flight. Late night. Last sigh sounded like a muttering-something like a clenching of dendrites to keep a memory safe: you forget the contents, their context, but you remember this scar, and how it is your body becomes ruptured by time.

You give up writing the book again. This surprises no one. You are moving back across the country, a reverse migration; you learned that from Bhanu—you learned to unmake yourself into a poetry comprised of sentences. How they want to paragraph themselves into a form of airport: departure terminal zero, now boarding capricious somnambulists, coyote visions, terror matrixes, ascensions, and burials. Into the blood stream: there you quiet every after.

The book is never finished; you read the book while I'm ripping it off my wall, pouring kerosene into a heap of paper and yarn—I start a small fire as you crack the spine; we coexist at a point of evacuation; the book escapes the fire. I give up writing the book shortly after you finish reading the book, now ruptured by an argument in its center. The book falls apart as you're reading it. Or my life falls apart in reverse.

The sentence structures fails to sustain the image—too weak for time—the cabin pressure drops a dream memory waking—holding space for spilt water instead.

Is it raining where you come from?

Is it raining right now?

I stitch together the sounds of rain to form another hum.

I sleep in this one and tell no one of the injuries I hold.

I return effervescent to vanish, but the image remains.

I can't realistically open this door—to escape; I'm here.

I know the flight never happened; maybe we crashed.

I stop writing the book and go back to sleep,

Time stain: death, worn within the body—the house is on fire and I am trying to write "a novel." I keep returning to water to write. Language continues condensing, vanishing subjects; subjects do not disappear. I grew them inside my body—burials tunneled down through atlas vertebrae, may have built a house there. Maybe formed an organ. I dug out Cinnabar pebbles from it—a mineral might keep you safe while other stones dream; others might lead the way to where you are going: the orchard the orchard the orchard: the: ocean.

In my whimsy, I forget which section this language goes into. I get drunk off the dream of it: the dream of dreaming something worth reading; to keep returning to a space in hopes it will hold itself together without you: that is an orchard; that is an airport: the ability to designate a state of distance, with a language that becomes independent of your own language. You lose the state of being before it's begun - you fumble your papers at the gate; the book becomes rearranged: remember: you threw the manuscript across the airport floor; someone yelled you were a terrorist - you dropped your notes and ran for the nearest set of stairs. The rearrangement found you in dreams.

You tried to make a book out of that: feeling/failing.

Lungs pirouette into absent

memory:

fingerprints glide toward an arm(;)rest. Before dark coffee burns a remarkable point into a moment. Before after, when then, stilling: the vacancy arises. Time continues without a concept of itself. I don't know when/how this flight will end.

Time spreads across the orchard, empty; in the distance, the dark ocean below blooms a neural grid. The book stops responding; nothing is working.

Out the window: dim clouds resemble the Spirit Quartz in my pocket; I forget which continent we're flying over. I forget the sentence and start again.

Glimpse a fractal eternity that accompanies a choice: step through a portal. Prepare(d) to exit.

Candlewax in rainfall: red cement kept cracks of citrus skin, harboring la noche en su piel. I keep returning to notebooks after the book has failed: it's clear there's not enough.

Note: there is no proper way to prepare for evacuation.

The flight ends suddenly; you wake up next to this book, on this page. Hello, I held this pocket of time for you while you slept. Here's some rose tea, or better yet: here's some rose petals for your coffee. Don't worry so much.

A Xix of Time

I dreamt of you

Becoming a Xix

As he named me

To be a Xix of Time.

Xix became a body

<table>
<tr><td>[became</td><td>a</td><td>family]</td></tr>
<tr><td>[became</td><td>a</td><td>tunneling]</td></tr>
<tr><td>[became</td><td>a</td><td>moment]</td></tr>
<tr><td>became</td><td>a</td><td>corpse</td></tr>
<tr><td>[became</td><td>a</td><td>caption]</td></tr>
<tr><td>[became</td><td>a</td><td>dirge]</td></tr>
<tr><td>[became</td><td>a</td><td>before]</td></tr>
<tr><td>became</td><td>a</td><td>memory</td></tr>
<tr><td>[became</td><td></td><td>anterior]</td></tr>
<tr><td>[became</td><td></td><td>absent]</td></tr>
<tr><td>[became</td><td></td><td>dreamt]</td></tr>
<tr><td>became</td><td></td><td>orchard</td></tr>
<tr><td>[became</td><td>a</td><td>notebook]</td></tr>
<tr><td>[became</td><td>blue</td><td>light]</td></tr>
<tr><td>[became</td><td></td><td>roses]</td></tr>
</table>

(to) become: dzonot.

Two earth bound bodies lay side by side gripping a peripheral gulf, eyes on sky.

These bodies might represent a family.

One exiting, one entering the house on fire as per the mandatory evacuation of biologies upon corpsehood.

The older body fresh from fugue breathes deep against a white cotton shirt. All sandals are off.

It's 3 a.m. when we arrive to the coast. We do not arrive so much as   pause.
You have to see how far the ocean has come – said a body bound to me by biology, we were after all, a family. Gulf sand conforms to arches and produces a European window I look through. Sweat paints the skin of all bodies present.

One wore white.

One did not.

I put my shoes in a plastic bag.

We lay in proximity, close enough to hear the larynx function, against gravity.

The vacuum was clear away from the sandbar strip.

There were negative ions lessening the anxiety of heart rhythms–the sway, the moon, the muscle tissue, loosening. The sand conforms to the body; the body conforms to the dimensions of the space upon which it is held/remembered–the sand is still warm–the water, a liquid twin.

Two bodies bearing similar imprints of time.

One white-haired, the other night-headed.

Both bodies experience sky.

First:

There is a dim

Then there is a bright,

The puncture mark arcs;

No bodies react aloud.

I forget why I'm telling you any of this. I wake up next to an emergency exit in Colorado, where the novel failed and festered into something else. The edges became viole(n)t; my blood turned in on itself and formed small fires in my liver, esophagus, and arteries - I drank to put them out; I wake up in America, on a bus towards the site of an accidental suicide, or maybe I'm on my way to the hospital again–the landscape smudges and fades with my heavy breathing, sighs the size of mountains–my sternum collapses in on my chest, and a language fills the absence like water. I make up (for) lost time declining madeleines in favor of feeling out a fringe narrative, noticing where the continuity fades into a matter of trust: *Remember, I'll fall with you if I can't catch you.* I become a vacuum for you to night.

The flight breaks down to its base components; it is safety I seek, here in the aisle way corridor of what's missing. I return to writing to keep myself alive; I tell no one of this. I wanted you to know that there is a truth behind all this hallucination, even if you don't believe (in) me. It's true.

There is only so much you can ruin before you're forced to renew. What this revisiting from the future that never happened is for– why the book I wrote is not the book you read–that book is as dead as my grandfather: dead as all the stars above the Gulf, where whale sharks weave water. Movement between timelines has caused a subtle rupture; we wade through a wake of intersecting futurities.

How will I know to find you in an airport or empty orchard
while a plane is planet pointed, as I sleep through gravity?

How will I find you when I arrive?

The water of a dzonot does not move; they are connected by their silence; less than half of their subterranean components have been mapped by man. They exist connected to dreams, mirror corridors to another stillness. Pyramidal neurons calcify light to awaken the quiet of a mountain peak; there is no river of Lythe in Yucatec mythology. Time is unending and cyclical. The water mimics the cosmos and leads into itself, eventually becoming a warm and buoyant void: a pinch of ocean otherwise known as gulf: Xibalba has many mouths.

Departure: sometimes the heart drops to a waltz, forgetting
something; altitude as recall mechanism:

I occupy a continent within my body.

I am going there today to bury my grandfather.

Asleep in a seat between two bodies I do not recall.

We are waiting—here above the planet tracing the cusp of time

with our stillness—while higher still I am a cup of (cold)

coffee trying to write field notes for my grandfather in

the event I see him again in dream(s). The moment when the

sun is under me. The moment the pituitary gland fires DMT.

To breach what may have started: dzonot.

I want to remove my grandfather from my grandfather

and become that other stillness.

Somnambulism(s) III

To continue from before Xix:

Oceanic heart in the earth of the orchard; I waited until the salt separated from the water. I kept it with me. I keep it safe.

I dreamt the orchard had grown wild with distance; the avocado trees outgrew the warehouse walls; the palms were all cactus now. There were white flowers everywhere. I buried him there. In the night of my heart.

While between sounds and phrases, I often feel I might burst apart. There is a terrible urge to cry, urn-like and unexpected. Gooseflesh cotton sigh. Eyes pointed west.

I want to carve a song of longing.

I find myself inverted in (my) dream space. It seems as though sleeping lumps hazy sentences together and shivers against the sound of my heart, muttering in its sleep.

A shard of Quartzite to my skin, formed a vestibule; I could not stop the movement; the wind continued.

My grandmother *Mama*, can't reach the avocados on the highest branches—renegade parrots and insects pick them off, or they fall dim and rot.

I dug 3 holes near a tree that grew berries black as earth midnight; that tree has become a stump now, reaching the sky requires far more digging.

I buried my grandfather between the palm trees in the black of the orchard, beneath a then.

It's snowing outside. I continue marking my thighs with Quartzite. Maybe this is a map.

I dreamt we were floating towards each other in the abyss.

I sent you a pocket of time that held what we had forgotten. It was a deep and painful blue that never quite healed. It left a mark, left a continent floating somewhere in the larynx of my heart; it's where I keep you safe.

¿Te acuerdas?

Eyes (may) focus inwards towards trace remnants of light and sound. Transcribe structure: temporary. I think of language like that. Temporary. Language is an approximate rendition of perception.

I dreamt you read that.

Xix would water the roses of my youth until he died; outside, we would discuss light, ideas of death and god and now, these images are so far away—I can't hold the wor(l)d—I don't recall the color(s) of his breathing, only that he did.

To extend a river of running from ocean to mountain.

I rest my head on the writing. I hear bodies enter and exit the sun. I remember holding some of them with my eyes, the way they fell away from me with time.

The aguacate tree grew heavy with fruit; the branches lowered, becoming other stumps; I water the orchard with small vials of memory from wherever I am.

What is not presently occurring:

I keep waiting for "the novel" to arrive. I keep waiting for a lighting strike to bring me shimmering visions of a complete funnel, to connect the time-cone diagrams inside of me to the streaming I might have stumbled upon. I keep waiting to remember.

Unbearable confusion. You wake up without reference. Waiting to arrive: a figure is slowed down, lowered, not yet falling.

I left a map on the face of a Labradorite slab; the continent blooms iridescent blue in a sea of golden lamplight, lit from below.

When the Quartzite touched me, I knew where to go.

The continent grew from under my skin and stitched me closed.

Are you ready to go (now)?

Ke'ext'aan Náay Eek

1. Split the hydrogen from the oxygen and inhale the separation. Add a bit of salt. Determine whether or not to examine the corpses of your dreams; examine the remnants anyways; depart from sense; find yourself (in) forgetting. The movement preceding your present is nowhere to be found and yet, here you remain.

2. The moaning of dissociative heart pacified by a blue, water soaked sponge. All he said was "Cha" (Ja' = water), "Na'at "(understand)? No one did. I think he wanted to return "Naay" (home).

3. Salt was used by the Yucatec Maya as a means of preserving food, the dehydration would allow for an added longevity that was not previously available to the corpses in the area. You can use salt to wash crystals and stones; to clean glass stained by dark time. Salt has a way of making things clear.

4. I poured salt across your rotting body at the first sign of rain. What would you do?

5. To collect salt, the inhabitants of the Peninsula would draw out large sections of land to capture ocean; to dry out the sea in hopes of crystal remedies. I keep a jar of ocean water next to me as I dream. I drink from it to remember what I cannot grasp.

Aisle memory: I waited for a body to return from beneath the earth. I skimmed time lines, zoning out the particularities of location. I learned to make a map from what I lost.

I keep stealing from airplanes. I want to keep up with the emergency procedures. I want to be ready for when I am falling down. A 737 has 6 emergency exits. But how does one escape the writing? How do I find the orchard?

I go digging for it. I tie plastic bags to bits of dead paper. They burn. From under. I am writing this from below an airport. Below the aircraft I catch bits of strangers, their life striated in my eyes as they depart the(ir) vessel(s).

The sun remained still after its motion had decayed. Some might call this wind; in other languages, this might be a whisper from the dead, whistling antes, *eeeeeeeeeeeeeeeeeeeeeee eeeeeeeee*

I perform bibliomancy with old notebooks to approach "a point" of emergence. Horizontal. The body is sleeping,

"the comma is where you turn the corner,"

Beneath the avocado orchard, a valley aquarium: trees grown from Yucatán seeds—he: my grandfather, taught me to dig deep holes. Line them with plastic bags: preservation membrane to be filled with faucet water. Pour a pen in it.

"Where might you be now?"

The halogen makes you nauseous, like anticipation, or love. You want to be afraid of flying - the altitude - its temperature. But you are not afraid. You are not flying. You are living.

Dzonots of light blossom in the distance; the bruise becomes a portal, a site of rich nutrients from which a body of night might feed feral dreams.

These portals are connected by the void that holds them.

I go running away from the city to reach a Quartzite point.
I lick my arm. I put my tongue upon the point and wake up.

At times the orchard is heaving in an asthmatic glow. Running until your chest bursts; there was once a structure to the itinerant migration of a lonesome heart, I ate it with a half a lemon. A touch of salt. I waited.

Translate: "I buried salt beneath the orange tree:"

1. Dig out a depression in the earth; allow the absence to fill you with its shape.

2. Continue breathing.

3. Deposit the night-reside of dream or lack there of. Fill the space with nothing. Continue breathing.

4. Speak aloud the following, as I learned from Bhanu Kapil; she speaks this from a mountainside, somewhere in India (as you read this): *Je n' existé pas. Je ne jamais existé pas.*

Nor will I ever.

What is this memory about? What is an orchard?

This is (not) an orchard: you build a sequence to build a meaning. Produce a pattern through which perhaps a sliver of sensation may be felt—a touch of something other than language—something that smells of salt, and blood. This may be similar to dreaming.

The act of dreaming, the way it was experienced:

Some dizzy night spun peonies out of poppy seeds; an ant swarm burst out of my head and led me to red threads of night—following images and signs until the morning—I wake up no longer certain I am (not) dreaming. This fabric seems real. But so does the flight.

I wake up dumping the contents of my backpack out to find nothing but sand and shells and conches; I say listening, "I always carry the ocean with me." I wake up, with all my notebooks drenched.

Aisle memory: dim lights droop the eyes while in flight; a lowly blue buzz of electricity marks the spine of the aircraft. This is meant to make you feel safe. This is meant to help with dreaming.

I spent several months in airports attempting to attempt to leave; I could (not).

I fail to write the orchard, I

transcribe my dreams instead:

Something like a mound of aguacates beset by a lemon patch. A smile of mud where a hole once was. Crushed containment packets lose their oxygen preceding the flight. Some eyes see better while sleeping.

Sleep collapses the roses, makes animals of memory; they ruptured linearity in favor of forgetting. I burrow until it's red.

Until I was certain. The orchard. The orchard. The Orchard.

I don't remember the orchard—just the hum in fog; scent of citrus blossoms, the flesh of the avocado made visible via animals; our bodies in relation. Sun as moon. White hair. Him, watering the orchard, coming home from a graveyard shift, coming from home from the terminal, Yucatán; leaving for the hospital, losing the language, leaning on Maya speak; asleep,

I remember the day I watched him die before he died.

I came to give him water from home. Still had to go back to the Yucatán. This time to find the quartzite tunnel; the dzonot dragon beneath his sister's house; I kept trying to find a narrative. I keep trying to form: narrative. I keep trying to write a "novel." I fail. I haunt the broken frame. I wipe the missing picture clean. I hold. I. I remember the lost light in a slumped face, giving up without the words to. I watched him quit. He didn't believe in my narrative(s) of airports and night coasts. I saw it in him: the way it could (never) be. I keep his look with me. I don't want to remember it as clearly as I do. I want to remember smiling. But one isn't always smiling.

I buried him in the orchard: a breathing continent adrift within a tract of skin. Pulmones llenos de água viva; la soledad de la boca de mi Corazón, lengua dormida, lleno de recuerdos y palabras y cuando se murió; vi, como su alma no podía mantener el negocio de tiempo. Tiempo es como piel; rotura es posible. ¿Quieres regresar? Naay, Náay, Káas Eek' Eek' Eek' Eek'.

I can't.

That's not supposed to be (t)here.

I press(ed) a shard of Quartzite to my left thigh.

Until red.

Xix: a Dzonot (Coyote Notes Set to Satie's 3 Gymnopédies)

I

I woke up; I washed cups—was washed up while in dream:

I woke up clean,
wearing white.

In the Yucatán, people wear white as a way to conduct light and become small breathing mirrors.

Seeing a body exit station,

Stepping outside of glass doors—the air is hot—I remove my shoes. I feel soil under sky; I start running (for it).

I run until my soles recognize soil; I keep running.

I hear a faint orange pitch pulling me forward, smudging;

entangled:

(eeeeeeeeeeeeeeeeeeeeeeeeeeeeeeeeeeeeeeeeeeeeeeeeeeeeeee)

II

I am a feral Kunzite coyote under a pink sky. Sweat stings eyes, makes all things snow-cloud-blur; muscles leak lemon aches, I run chasing echoic slaps of foot on path—a pueblo rises from wavering heat, everywhere green;

I am where my grandfather grew.

(I am home)

ahead of me: a crowd of mirrors gathers the conches.

Mama tends to the orchard beyond Xix, she who is the orchard and its keeper, builds an altar every day. She gathers her roses to spell Xix; she leaves a glass of water, slices of avocado; she levels the sound of the ocean with her singing, recalling Pedro Infante in his Yucatán front yard, she keeps watering the orchard beyond all of us, maintaining the moonlight, dimming the leaves. She forms dzonots from her dreams and by morning, she pours them into the orchard, for safekeeping. She becomes a mirror, becomes a moon, to hum a deep song to open the continent; the conches sing.

III

I walked until I stood.

I stood until I held

until.

I felt body oscillate, shivering until skin shed.

And then, light:

Earth opened up behind my grandfather's smile
Eyes crinkled the way mine do now

30,000 ft.

I watched him fall backwards as the land creased,
Until I could not see him, or remember his laughter

20,000 ft.

I watched, falling with him. Bodies in binary:

Eucalyptus leaves

15,000 ft.

the pencil fell out my teeth; I was harbored by my

howl(ing)   between bodies,

asleep

13,000 ft.

Water was soon rushing from all bodies present; the ground shimmered. It moved inwards where two bodies became:
after.

10,000 ft.

light-flood shoots up from breeched earth; where bodies fell, they sank; no sound of bottom heard.

5,000 ft.

I shut my eyes for fear of losing:

this:

There were no mirrors gathered there any longer, the image now clear:

A dzonot to drink from

2,000 ft.

I dip my palms down past the dzonot horizon

500 ft.

I cup a word of water to my lips and drink:

_______________.

Appendix II: Oneirology
A (pre/post) Flight Field Manual

ZIP CODE

VIA AIR MAIL

GELI,

JETU

XIX

Hannah paints the book before it's finished; she tells me, *I'm sorry there's no airplane in the ocean reflection, but there just couldn't be, because the flight never happened*—she says this and I return to it.

You need to know that my hope here is to dream with you while living, to split reality while reading: see, I've worked hard to produce a torn pigment of *now.*

Might it someday inhabit your wrist?
Like this: timepiece, cicatrix, or aisle memory?

I don't need language to know my body. The flight fidgets and shakes as the depth of sky folds in on itself, revealing a vacuum. I keep coming home in hopes of finding you there, waiting to be something else with me. I lied. I stopped looking. I gave up and returned to the core of the animal: nomadic orbit. I left my first write. I left my all behind. In the airplane, I watch a trace of being depart(ed). To be alive with the knowledge that I have died, somewhere else. I step from behind my seat and reveal that there is no one here. And you don't remember talking to yourself. The aloud becomes a distant whisper. The brightness of the overhead, a dim night; neurons below the aircraft are firing and giving way to dreams of light. I almost forgot about the hand signals that take place upon the act of flying. "Pretend to give us your attention." Yes, please. Won't you? You'll need this when waking up. See, there are no exits on this flight. No lights. The blue from above descends like a collapsing roof or chimney. Here we are safe from earthquakes, though, we feel the sky shake. We feel the sky shake from the depths of the desert, asleep below an ocean of oxygenated light; the Saguaro cacti whisper hums from the floor of the flight. The desert is here with you. Or, I am here with you. I want to return to a state of staying still. We move like a wildfire and oh. There you are, out the window, reversing the trajectory. We're spinning. I wake up on an airplane above the Rockies; I spread out and consume the language. Memoria fracazado makes me cry hablando de los cuerpos del mar, y el Cielo is a kind of ocean. I didn't realize we would be here for so long. I keep going about my day(s) moving forward, moving forward; moving forward. Walking through the ruins of my youth; recalling fossil memory: I was a snake, or was born a snake. The keeper of a dzonot. My head a horse. My feathers mirrors. My heart a dark portal. I enter Xibalba and return with memories of the future. I'm running through the forest to the ocean. My body is naked. My body has died. This is the memory of a ghost running from its body (in)to the ocean. Or. I wake up on the flight again. Between this and living I'm not sure I'm ever arriving. The altitude does something to the writing; does something to the being writing or operating as the function of writing. What is the function of writing?

To return (home).

From above the earth we witness the vast blank expression of time, disappearing. The power goes out in the house you grew up in. You fail to grow up. You fail to return; instead, you wake up on this flight, reading this book by an animal you don't know; I washed my paws before coming aboard; did you do the same? I burned my wrist opening my body in the desert. I broke my toe in Tucson. I opened portals with bodies of light. Andrea taught me to think like a magi. I'm (always) learning to be alive, turning myself inwards. I know where to find it. The desert of my heart, I bury the night sky; I catch a pack of stars before they depart—I warp the time surrounding them and fashion a pocket of neurons to catch the descent—I don't want to forget, how we forget—Do you remember your first sunrise? DJ tells me about watching the sun rise at 40,000 feet, the mountain it formed. A disembodied voice says it's going to be pretty bumpy going down. Fasten your seatbelt. Return the trays to their upright and locked position. We are traveling at 517 miles per hour. 38,871 ft above the earth, still within the earth, learning how it is we open to the moment above the continent; to welcome the turbulence. This brings you home. Forget your fear of flying. Forget your being alive before this. We woke up here together, scared in the dark with turbulence near by, or approaching–are we always approaching? Approaching the site of our own death. How we become something like life. To know and then continue. I subscribe to the catch and release program of thoughts. Listen to what's come up from below. Proprioception: your body has become a station of light; we have become an angle of grief in repose, learning how to repair itself. The body holds memory holds us still while we shiver and cry at night; we write and the body contracts/we writhe and the body becomes. Turbulence sets in. First like a California earthquake—did it really happen? I guess we'll wait for the news, or a family member to ask: did that just happen? Was that real? How we know "real" is based in hermetic detail. The pilot sees beyond the cockpit; I see the dream catch fire. I pray to put it out. To put it underground. How do you bury a now? How do you bury a noun? You carry it with you. I carry you with me. The manuscript has been digging holes in my back from the crack of its spine, I designed a failure to function, only to learn I didn't want it to fail. I deposited the body of my heart into the crook of the sky; I went looking for corners with the long light of redeyes and did not stop until I was tarmac. I was a brick of time tossed across an architecture—smashed on impact. I unpack the contents of my heart and let them dry along the coast. I caught a glimpse of the flight: a bright fiery lemon trailing lines like shadows, showing where we've been or come from; the aircraft emanates a lavender light; I guess we are a type of sun. My Eek', in the moment beneath your own, there is a receding sense of the future. The past comes to greet you; coexistence can be a problem. Superimpositions are common—the blurring makes you dizzy, or distorts your dreams in such a way that you read this. The tension of the timelines collapses comet, uncovering the earth; planting Xibalba, allowing us access. I smashed the airport into the soil, until I could locate the sky by looking at my skin. I want to offer you time to find time to make time to waste time outside the window. I wonder where you are when you read or hear these words. Determine the language and start again. I write my body that I might open. The x-ray reveals stones and scaffolding. The boarding pass disappears in the radiation. We are 75 miles away. The turbulence is as bad as you want it to be. Catch/release a sense of gravity; learn to see that this (wreading) is floating. Or finding. I think it's closer to finding the floor of your notebook somewhere in your body. And you're tired. And it's been a long day, the nows piled up and became befores prior to boarding. But you're here now. Your phone is dead or in don't "crash the plane" mode. Shhh, Rest. I want you here. I'll gather the conches. I'll rest alongside you—the altitude is coming, or already here. Lightheaded sleep brings you to a series of awakenings. In 21 minutes, we will encounter/discover/create the earth. I need you to be sitting upright. I need you to breathe with me. Here, use the word "lungs" there. Breathe like a tiger. Hannah is teaching me how to soothe the dead, or the memory of them and their ongoing goings-on. Below us a nexus of electric light and sound surmises the town of "I know where we are." But here we are, we are here but, something has changed. We have changed. We wake up separated by time and space. We wake up pining for the other without language. We emanate light. We call out across the void with a song composed of rose-colored vibrations. I bring my body to the foot of the page and tear open a portal; peel back the flesh and write away, we begin to wake together. You there and I here–a sphere of time zones and heartbeats. I break my heart that I might love you as I love Xix, who is gone but still roaming with(in) me. There it is. I am sending you a deep star. I'm writing you a dark ocean. I'm prepping the orchard for your arrival. Stay as long as you'd like—keep waking up, practice your dreaming, dear somnambulist—learning how to walk again in the redwood forest, for the first time, in a frenzy.

Luminous Details From The Archive

(2012-2015)

a + i = m[illegible]ing field : *iron Filings

memory

Forgetting

a = Forgetting

i = memory

radiant

Future

Encounter

convergence

drift dimensions

Present.

negative luminescence

- observations - Simultaneous attraction + Repell -

does not memory function this way?

a node calling forward to time

and yet, the motion of the body

Resisting the reversal of Recall -

Feral memory - Body memory

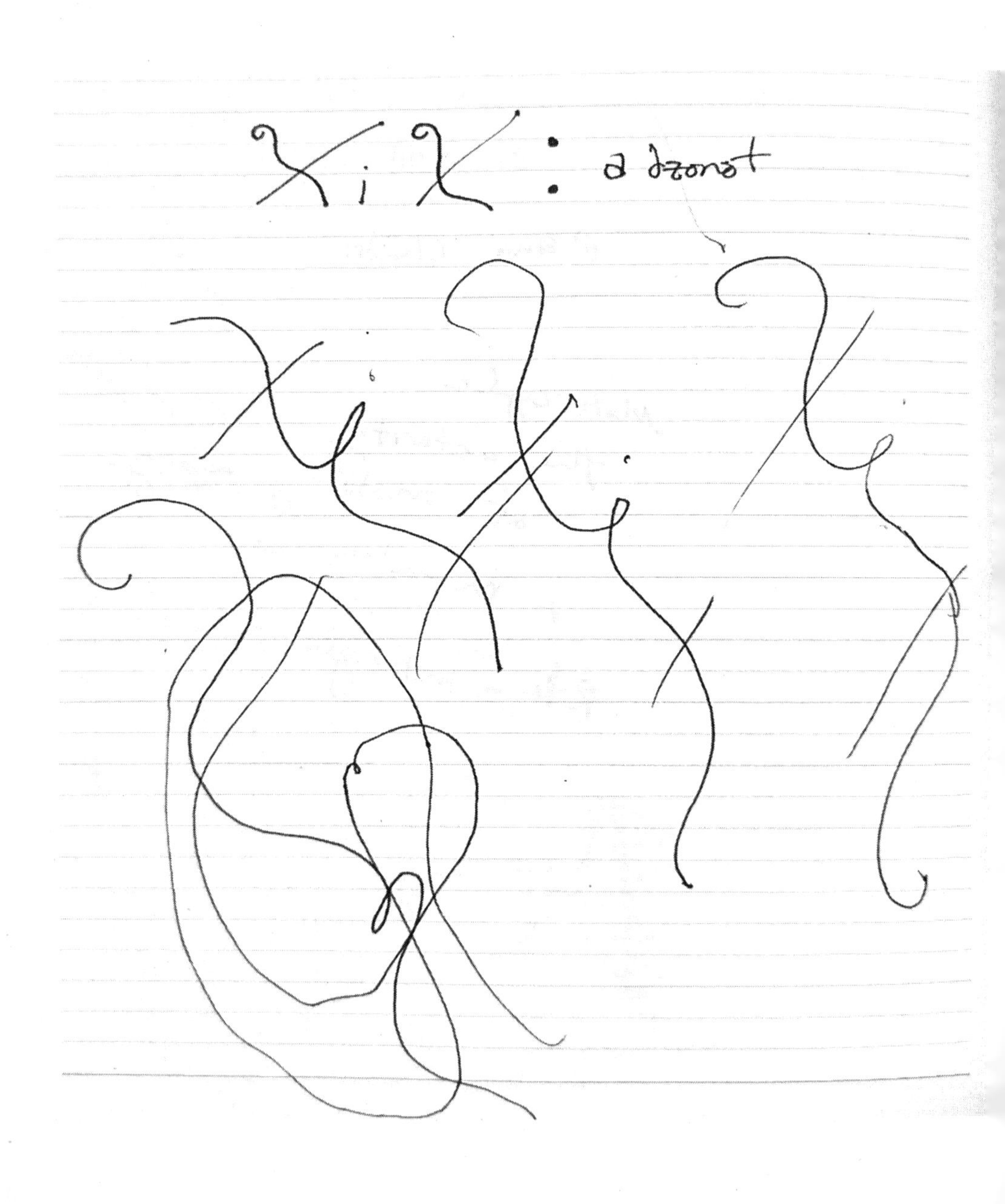

How is it that all which haunts me
is me?

It's me losing my day.
It's me getting wandering stuck.
It's me making me crazy.

And yet.
the day is not mine.
This skin is Eczema-ridden
space dust.

I am noone. Know nothing.
lilting trash in Space.

I,
keep getting stuck in the soup of time.
Stuck in the constant traps of structure.
trapped by being anything at all.

every Eye
A DZONOT.

Connected.

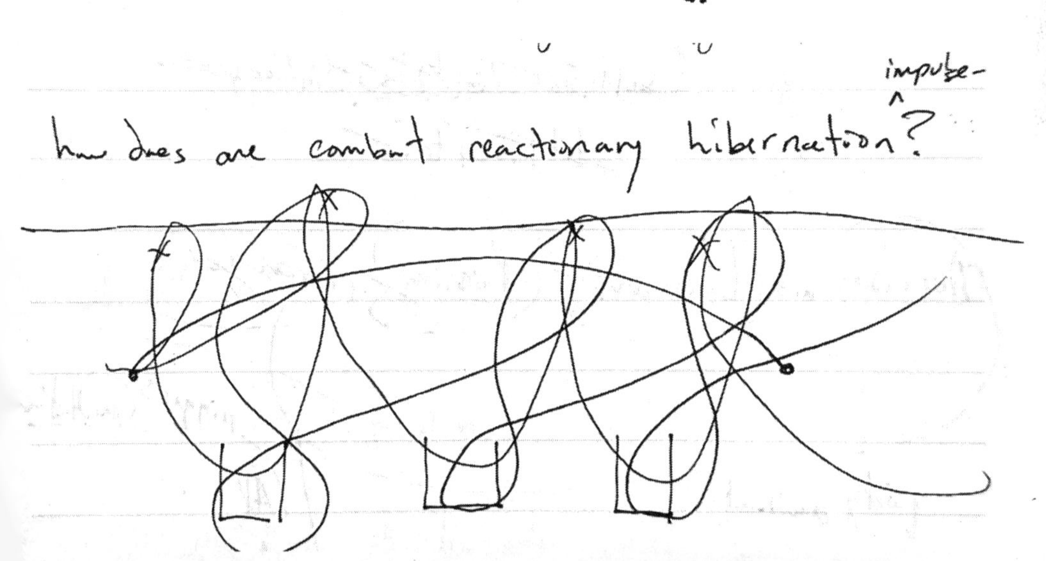
how does one combat reactionary hibernation impulse?

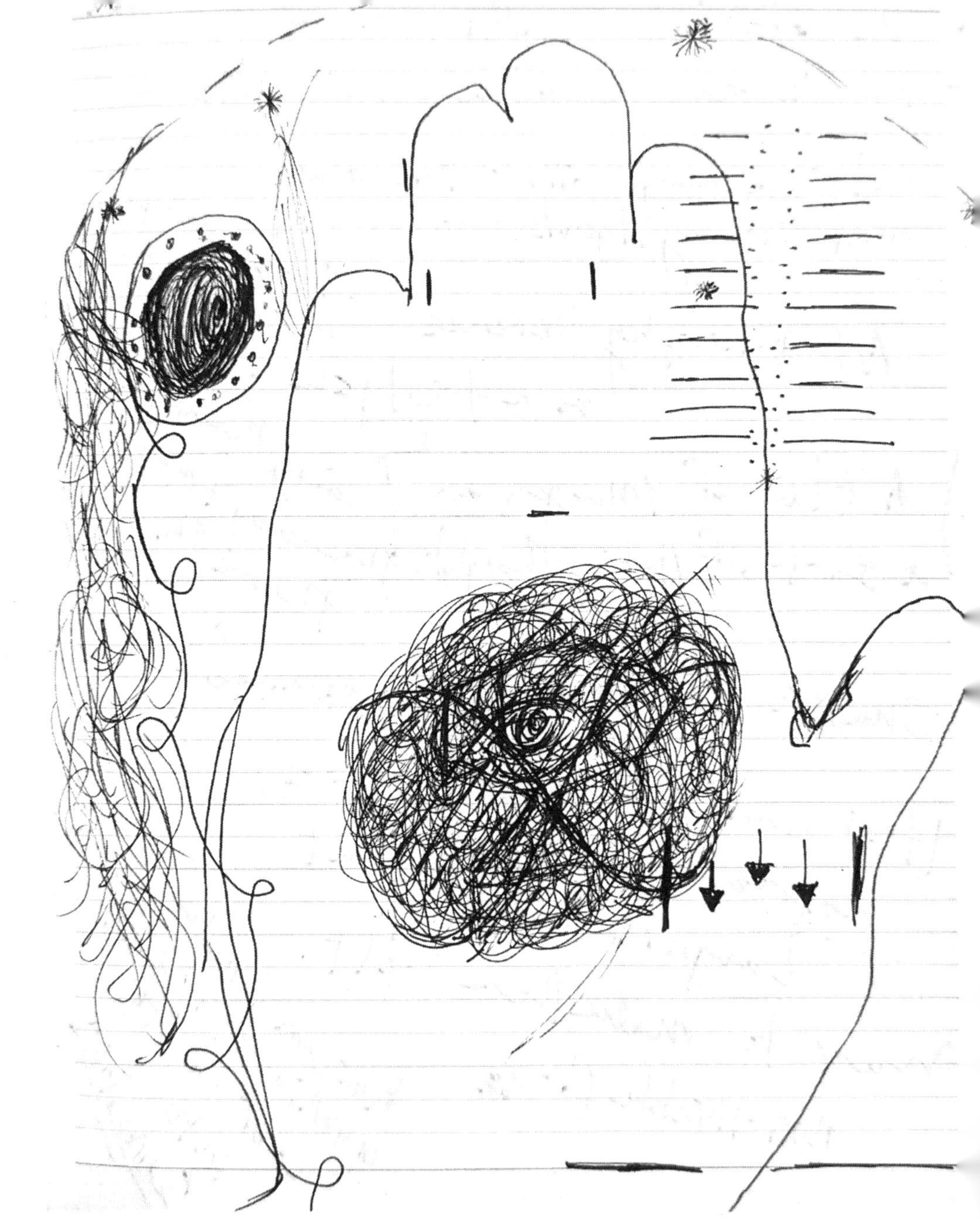

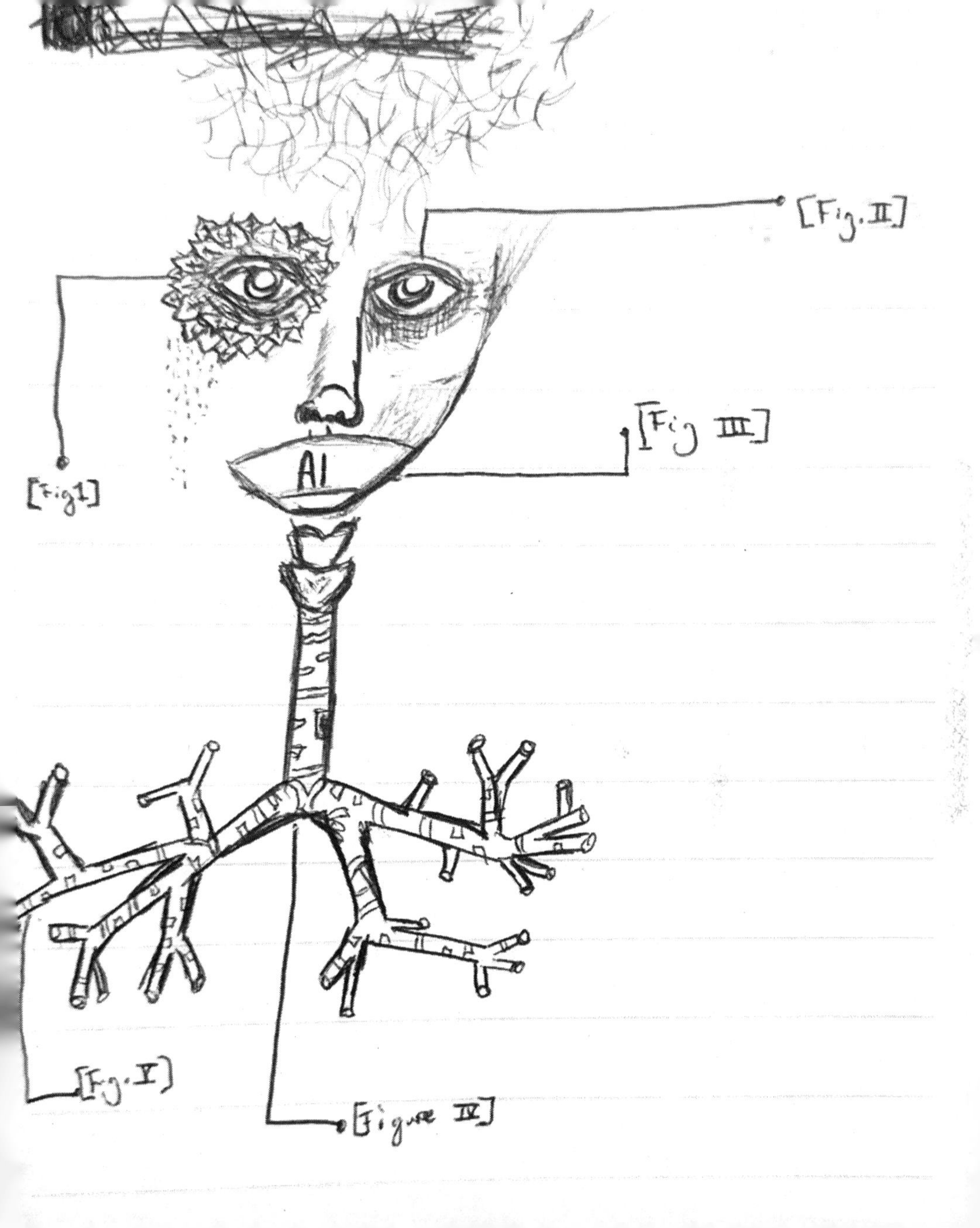
[Fig.II]
[Fig III]
AI
[Fig1]
[Fig.V]
[Figure IV]

Don't Forget.

here i am writing (as top soil) : below " w/in me

this is thinking narrative mechanism for accessing

(the airplane) a flight

occuring and yet not

and yet, this drops off.

into memory

(it should be said this all occurs w/in the body its an alchemy of thinking of thought and language)

recall both voluntary and involuntary

and deeper still

dreamscape (has access to and relogged and strained through thinking)

yet where is this exactly?

all of this occurs w/in the body (as event)

All of this informed by being – what is being? – the buddha body of reality? the Bergsonian expression of consciousness –

i want to live now.

Grandfather you were a watchmaker — A dealer in gemstones & time
you taught me how the quartzite grown kept the time Alive —

This is a Quartzite bell to fill
with Black Lavender Milk — bring in "well-worn"

Dzonot Sagrado
Quartzite cave
memory / dream —

+ Downtown LA
jewelry + watch shop

i forgot my family is a family of jewelers

Sleep deprivation
hallucination
the flight
Dzonot Sagrado

Make a mandala for

(uglysketches)

Eye of the Duck
C.S. Giscombe

circuitry
a i

Absence or,
Forgetting: that
which connects us all?

al
i
a
al

magnetic
fields

the text

a=0

a=0

Moon
tongue

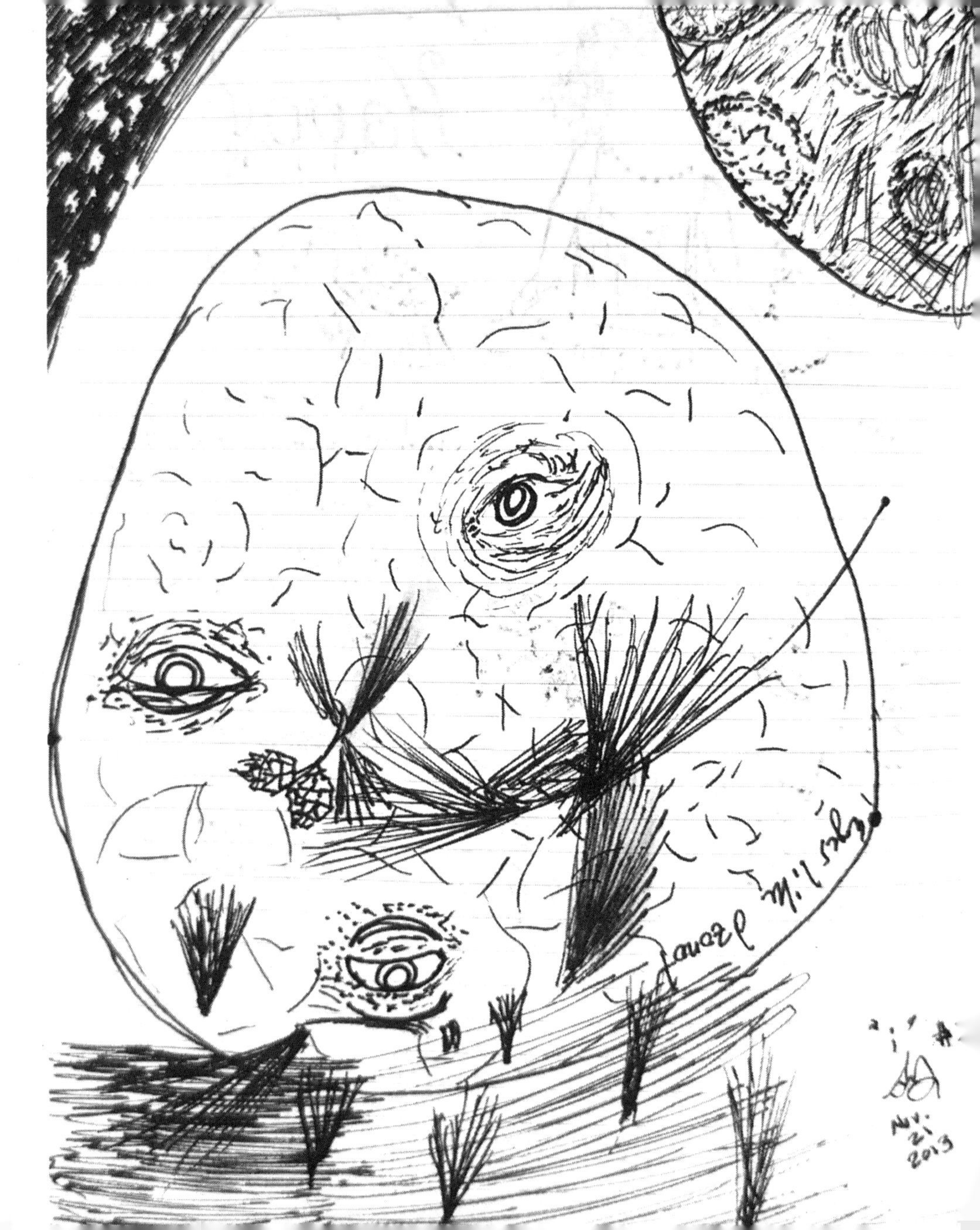
Nov. 21 2013

(naming) yucatan: i dont understand

Xix
Xan

(Sun dawn airport)

Mayan Lessons/ Forgetting

(what is an airport/plane?)

elephant story

Spain dreams

F

L

I

G

H

T

dzonot
dream

building cenotes
digging holes

(waiting bodies)

On ~~An~~ beach
Yucatan

Hospital

* Expand your idea of what an accomplishment is.
"i don't think of myself as having 1 voice." – HM

Make a list of things that make you happy.

* there is a difference between Revising and composing

Alfonzo lingis – : i need to see what i want to change" H

* Schedule days for yourself.

. come back at 3.

visual poetry experience

think about blank pages:
[walls : fences : trees : paths : stream]
snow : etc.
write on them
without polluting

w/out impermanent
+ Ephemeral.

Start w/a single word.
think of ways you could write
without leaving a permanent mark
Ephemeral trace: up to 6 words – max impact
6 – w/ different ...

circling – departure

trasit

awakening
@ the site of departu

– think: amnesiac diaries.

a

Dream

train station.

train

Dream

i

A Falling leaf does not begin in
on a branch, a falling
body does not begin
vertically.

Each existing

First in Air.

Somatic trauma theory -

Autobiography + contextual narrative -

you titrate the ~~dos~~ Ⓐ

the writing. ← the note book

inchoate elements

~~$~~ ossilation

the theory of

titration ⟵⟶ pendulation

how do make it shake?

ossilate -

begin @ the point it reaches to.

the thing that makes you shake anyways -

[A Invention]

"To achieve rancid nudity as a writer."

BK

This morning i woke up and decided to retrieve my manuscript from where i'd left it to die a week ago - the night of my 25th Birthday (Nov. 10th) I'd put together a reading/performance night at Colombia Cemetery in Boulder, CO - Colombia Cemetery was the first permanent cemetery in Boulder CO - We read by the "Beach" - a headstone of 3 residents that read Beach in large Capital text. The night was Domingo, Hannah, Mike, Joel Engl and myself with votives + candles wine bourbon a camera and a flood light. This morning it was, just me, my bag a tote bag for the manuscript and a book i was reading. I thought some one had thrown it away - small traces emerged - Flattened by the snow - its smell and the time it took me to retrieve it - i find purple threads and follow them to their extremities; BLM has become a Frozen monster - maybe dead. as i dig the carcass out of the Frozen earth - i can't help but be transported to earlier this year: A February Sunday spent digging in Emily Dickinson's garden with a plastic corkscrew determined to retrieve some of that earth - the earth upon which she walked - The ground was frozen then too.

suddenly...
i remember this
from a dream
long ago.

there are sounds here
that are not here.

Archive — arc ive are art / kt / arc hive

Access + the public space

[recieving dead space]

= dream memory

the line of the writer: a

line of (assumed) narrative: the plane: the flight.

* each ossilation is
a pendulation
implied *

dusk.

MEMORY

Dream

This ends w/ the plane descending.

- Suitcase contents:
Rosary (from Marion)
- Return flight ticket
  - from first trip w/ Xix
- Xix's notebook
  + Steinian verse
- Notebooks spanning 2011 – 2013
  - Shining woman tarot card
- Aircraft Evacuation notes
- tangerine skin w/ glitter
  - helped incubate book's end
- stick found while hiking w/ carl
- Avocado seed: durational experiment — Split in two.
  - a miniature exerpt of Bonny Pam
- dzonot instructions —

A pendulum moves forward (horizontally) / the forces / indexes of the event.

it's like a pulsing jelly fish — that's the flight — flashes of what are the particles of each concept? what are the quarks hidden/~~[illegible]~~ within.

A concept is a brick: it can be used to build a court house of reason, or it can be thrown through a window.

This table of elements = my bricks,

think ink, this brain are my cement,

by which i mean connectivity. space

fractions in this way to connect all the

Retinal adjustment reveals the shape of subject,

Following outlines, is gone before the image arrives.

the motion of a photon hitting glass/ event energy?

Rock in pond.

[What muscles are used in falling? most common accident from falling? injury?]

[What happens to the body when falling?]

Always approaching the horizon, never touching . . .

What a thing,
this: to be human.

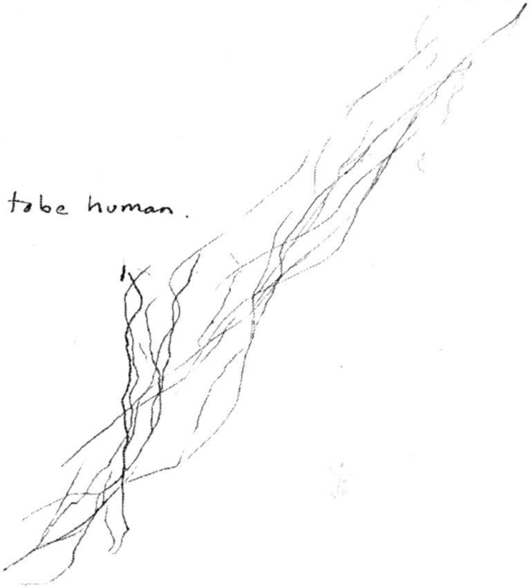

i dreamt you wrote something
in my notebook,
You finished a poem;
made one ocean.

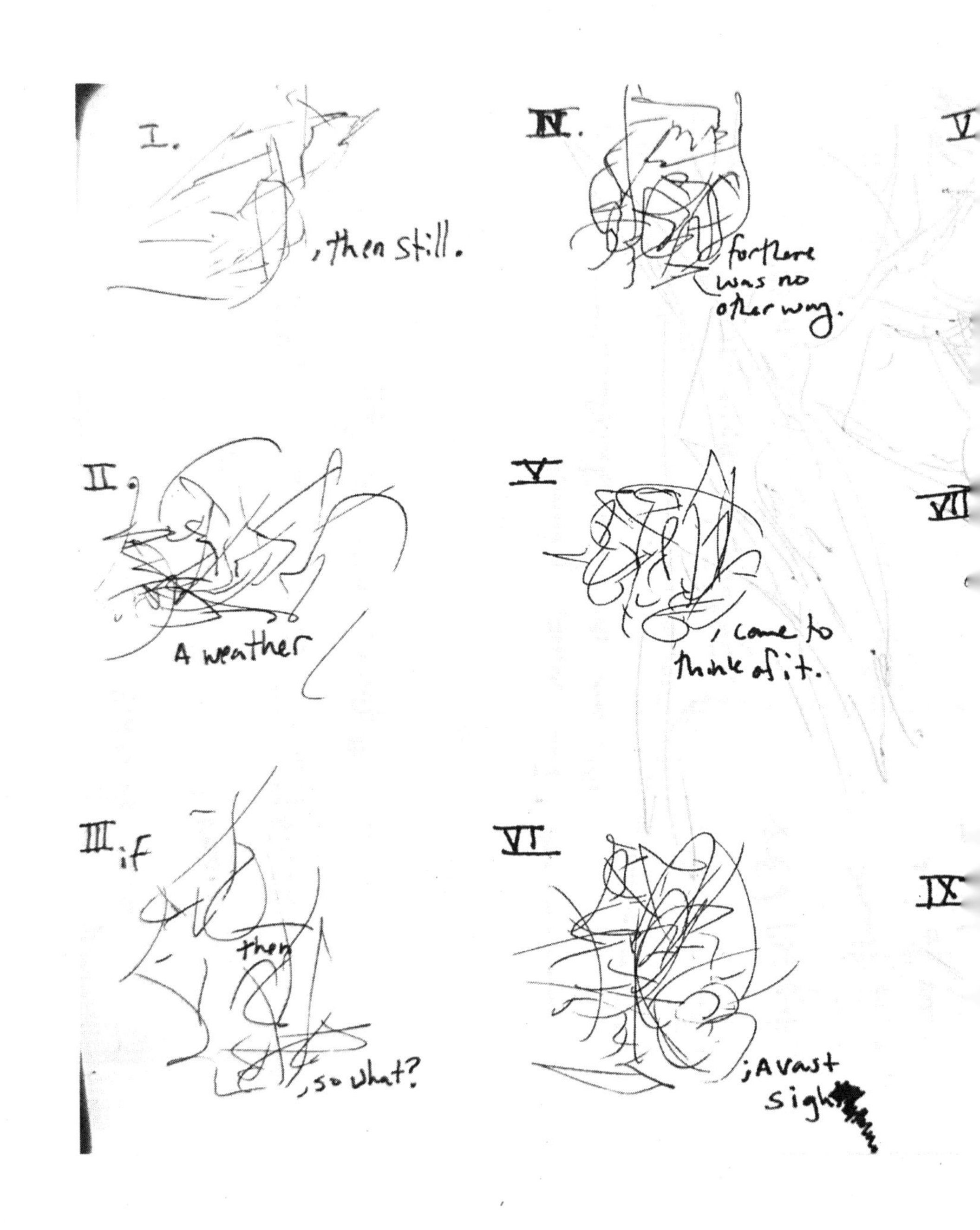
I.
, then still.
IV.
for there was no other way.
V
II.
A weather
V
, come to think of it.
VII
III. if
then
, so what?
VI
; A vast sigh
IX

X
time-limits
XI
Alone with it -
XII
humble,
something
like the body -

Exhaustion
Moon.